A DARK, DARK TALE

Ruth Brown

Andersen Press London
Hutchinson Australia

Once upon a time there
was a dark, dark moor.

On the moor there was
a dark, dark wood.

In the wood there was
a dark, dark house.

At the front of the house
there was a dark, dark door.

Behind the door there
was a dark, dark hall.

In the hall there were
some dark, dark stairs.

Up the stairs there was
a dark, dark passage.

Across the passage was
a dark, dark curtain.

Behind the curtain was
a dark, dark room.

In the room was a dark,
dark cupboard.

In the cupboard was
a dark, dark corner.

In the corner was
a dark, dark box.

And in the box there was... A MOUSE!